The Berenstain Bears
TRICK OR TREAT

Even little bears
expect a good fright
when they go out for treats
on Halloween night.

A First Time Book®

Random House 🏠 New York

Copyright © 1989 by Berenstains, Inc. All rights reserved under International and Pan-American Copyright Conventions. Published in the United States by Random House, Inc., New York, and simultaneously in Canada by Random House of Canada Limited, Toronto.

Library of Congress Cataloging-in-Publication Data:
Berenstain, Stan. The Berenstain Bears trick or treat / Stan & Jan Berenstain. p. cm.— (A First time book) SUMMARY: The Berenstain Bear cubs have an adventure on Halloween night that proves Mother's adage, "Appearances can be deceiving." ISBN: 0-679-80091-3 (pbk); 0-679-90091-8 (lib. bdg.) [1. Halloween—Fiction. 2. Bears—Fiction] I. Berenstain, Jan. II. Title. III. Series: Berenstain, Stan. First time books. PZ7.B4483Bfh 1989 [E]—dc19 89-30884

Manufactured in the United States of America   1 2 3 4 5 6 7 8 9 0

The sights and sounds of autumn were all around as Mama Bear pushed her shopping cart along the path that led to the Bear family's tree house.

The trees and shrubs were ablaze with color. Farmer Ben's pumpkins stood bright orange in the October sun. The crows cawed noisily as they searched the stubble for bits of corn. Wild geese in great V-formations honked high in the sky as they flew south.

But the surest sign of the season was inside the tree house hiding behind Papa Bear's easy chair. It was Brother Bear waiting to try out his Halloween costume on Mama. It wasn't Halloween yet, but Brother and Sister couldn't wait to try on their new costumes. Sister was going to be a beautiful ballerina. "Well, what do you think?" she asked, taking the third position.

"Shh!" said Brother. "Mama's coming!"
Brother had chosen to be a spooky monster
on Halloween. He had bought the spookiest
monster mask he could find, and Mama made
the rest of the costume.

"Boo!" he shouted as Mama came in with the groceries.

"Help! A monster!" she cried, pretending to be frightened.

"It's only me, Mama," he said, showing his face.

"So it is," said Mama. "Well, that just goes to show that appearances can be deceiving."

"Appearances can be deceiving—
what's that mean?" asked Sister.

"It's just a grown-up way of saying that
things aren't always what they look like,"
explained Mama as she unpacked the groceries.
"Look! Goodies!" said Brother.
"Hands off, please," said Mama. "Those
are for trick or treaters, who come
to our house tomorrow
night."

Brother and Sister were very excited about Halloween—and a little nervous, too. This was the first year they would be going trick or treating without a grownup along to supervise. "I'm not so sure I like the idea of them going by themselves," said Papa as he carved the pumpkin he got from Farmer Ben.

"It's pretty spooky out there,"
he added, making a scary face
at the cubs.

"Now, Papa," said Mama. "If Brother
and Sister want to accept the challenge
of going out on their own, I think we
should encourage them.

"But remember," she continued, turning to the cubs, "there'll be strict rules: you'll stay in your own neighborhood and you won't eat any of the treats until you're back home."

"Besides," said Brother, "we won't really be by ourselves. We made a trick-or-treat date with Cousin Freddy, Lizzy Bruin, and Queenie McBear."

"There!" said Papa, putting the finishing touches on the jack-o'-lantern. Then he lit a candle inside it and turned out all the lights. It was pretty scary.

The next day Brother and Sister began planning the trick-or-treat route they'd follow that night. Brother got a pencil and paper and made a map of the neighborhood. That way, he explained, they wouldn't miss anybody. "Let's see, now," he said, "we'll stop at our houses first—ours, Freddy's, Lizzy's, and Queenie's. Then we'll do Farmer Ben's and our sitter's— Mrs. Grizzle."

"Mrs. Grizzle, for sure," agreed Sister. "She usually makes special Halloween cookies."

"And Teacher Jane—she gives out good stuff. How about Dr. Grizzly?" asked Brother. "She's into health snacks."

"I think so—just to be polite," said Sis.

"Gramps and Gran, of course."

"Of course."

TRICK-OR-TREAT MAP

"I'll tell you one place we *are* going to miss," said Brother, folding his map.

"What place is that?" asked Sister.

"That one!" he answered, pointing out the window at the home of old Miz McGrizz. It was a spooky, twisted old tree house in a thicket at the end of Crooked Lane. "We're definitely not going there," he added with a shiver.

"Whyever not?" asked Mama, who was listening.

"Why not?" said the cubs. "Because she's a witch! That's why not!"

"What utter nonsense!" protested Mama. "True, Miz McGrizz is old and bent and rather forbidding looking. But I can assure you she's a perfectly nice person." But the cubs didn't believe her. Not for a minute. They knew better. *Everybody* knew better. No doubt about it, Miz McGrizz was a witch, for sure.

Just after dark, a pirate, a skeleton, and the Wicked Queen from Snow White came for Brother and Sister.

They were Freddy, Lizzy, and Queenie, of course, and together they ventured out into the darkness with their trick-or-treat bags.

Before they could get started collecting Halloween goodies, they were joined by some worrisome company: Too-Tall Grizzly and his gang, out for mischief. Too-Tall didn't waste any time trying to get Brother, Sister, and their friends to go along with him and his gang.

"Come on. We'll show you goody-goodies how to have some *real* Halloween fun," he said, pulling Brother along with him.

"What sort of fun?" asked Brother warily.

"Oh, you might say we're gonna put the trick back in trick or treat," he said, chuckling. It was so dark that Brother and the others didn't notice where they were heading.

"Hey!" said Sister. "This is Crooked Lane!"

"That's right," said Too-Tall. "We're gonna play a few tricks on old Witch McGrizz."

"W-what sort of tricks?" asked Brother. Her gnarled, twisted old tree house loomed ahead.

"First," whispered Too-Tall, taking a roll of toilet paper from his jacket, "we'll decorate her house with a little of this. Then maybe we'll tie a few knots in her clothesline. Then smear some honey on her broomstick so she'll stick to it when she tries to fly."

But before Too-Tall and his gang could start their mischief, the front door opened and a bright yellow light stabbed the darkness. And there in the doorway stood the frightening figure of old Miz McGrizz! "Aha!" she said in a gravelly voice. "I'm ready for you!"

She then led the terrified cubs into a cozy living room. To their great surprise, there was a big tray of beautiful candy apples all prepared for Halloween visitors.

"Mama was right," whispered Sister to Brother. "Miz McGrizz really *is* a sweet, kind old person!"

The cubs thanked her for the beautiful apples and went about the rest of their trick-or-treat business.

Later that evening Brother and Sister were at home looking over all the treats they had collected. The beautiful candy apples stood out, and Papa asked where they came from.

"From Miz McGrizz," answered Brother.

"From that scary-looking old grouch-puss that lives down Crooked Lane?" said Papa.

"That's right," said Brother, taking a delicious bite of his candy apple.

"You must really try to remember, Papa," said Sister, giving her apple a little lick, "appearances can be quite deceiving."